# A FAIRY KING

# Also by C. J. Brightley

**Erdemen Honor:**
*The King's Sword*
*A Cold Wind*
*Honor's Heir*

**A Long-Forgotten Song:**
*Things Unseen*
*The Dragon's Tongue*
*The Beginning of Wisdom*

**A Fairy King**
*A Fairy Promise*

# A FAIRY KING

C. J. BRIGHTLEY

Egia, LLC

ISBN : 1517152488

Published in the United Sates of America by Egia, LLC.

www.cjbrightley.com

*For my parents*

# ONE

Hannah woke with a start as the first ray of sunlight slanted across her face. It was a Saturday, and she was allowed to get up and watch cartoons if she was very quiet. It took a moment for Hannah to realize that she was staring at the very edge of an envelope some two inches from her nose.

She sat up, the worn blanket pooling softly around her slim legs. Nine years old, she was petite, with nut-brown hair that fell in soft curls down to her waist and wide gray-blue eyes. The girl was inclined to solemnness, not because she was sad, but because she was busy imagining adventures. Yet she had the resilient happiness of a loved child, undaunted by adult worries or grief.

Hannah turned the envelope over in her hands, examining it. She didn't know anything about stationery, but this felt expensive; the paper was thick and creamy, with a velvety feel against the soft pads of her fingers. It had no name or address on the front. After a moment, she carefully pulled the flap open and read the letter.

> *My name is Cadeyrn. I am nine years old, and I am writing this letter to practice my English. I hope it finds you well. What is your name? Where do you live? The name of the place I live would translate something like Land of Green Hills, but I think you would call it Faerie.*
>
> *My father is king here. That makes me the prince, and that means I have to study a lot. I have to know all the human languages, except for a few small ones that my father permits me to use magic to translate. I have to study swordplay and all kinds of magic. Do you have to study?*
>
> *I had better go. I hear someone coming.*
> *Please write back.*
> *Cadeyrn*

Could it be real? Faerie didn't really exist, of course. But *someone* had sent her a letter. The handwriting was a messy cursive, slightly neater than her own, and there was an ink blot near one corner. Studying it again, she detected a faint scent, and raised the paper to her nose. Yes, the ink, or perhaps the paper, had a faint, sweetish scent to it, not exactly sugar, not exactly floral, but some indefinable sweetness.

A sound by the window made her look up. On the branch outside, a large, white bird stared at her, his head tilted to one side.

Cartoons could wait.

She stepped out of bed, her little arms prickling in the cool air. She pulled her flannel pajama top over her undershirt and buttoned it, checking to make sure the buttons were in the correct holes, then stuck her feet into the fluffy kitten slippers she'd gotten for her birthday the previous week. In the kitchen she found a pad of yellow legal paper, her dad's preferred kind for making his ever-expanding list of planned home improvement projects. She found a purple pen in the junk drawer and sat at the kitchen table, her legs swinging.

> *Dear Cadeyrn,*
>
> *My name is Hannah. I live outside a big city called Philadelphia. We have snow in winter, but it's springtime now and all the snow has melted. My birthday was last week, and now I'm nine too. I have to study math and grammar and history at school. We're studying the Declaration of Independence. Do you know what that is?*
>
> *My mom will be home soon. She's a nurse. She helps people. I might be a nurse when I grow up, except maybe not because seeing blood makes my stomach feel like it wants to turn inside out. I have a dog named Fuzz. Do you have a dog?*
>
> *I would like to be your friend. Please write back.*
> *Hannah*

She frowned. How would Cadeyrn get her letter? Hannah had only a vague understanding of the postal system, but she did know that addresses were necessary. His envelope bore neither her address nor his. She folded the letter into a square and took it upstairs, where she left it on her desk. Then she went back downstairs and turned on the television, finding her favorite morning cartoon.

"Mom, how do you mail a letter to someone if you don't have their address?"

"You don't, honey. You need an address if the letter is going to get to them. Why?"

Hannah frowned. "But... what if it got to them anyway? Could that happen?"

"No, sweetheart. How would the mailman know where to take it?"

The logic was unassailable. She went back up to her room to reassure herself that the letter was real. It sat on her desk, one smooth sheet of paper neatly tucked back into the envelope.

With a sigh, she put her own letter into the top drawer in her nightstand.

She received another letter a week later.

> *Dear Hannah,*
>
> *I was told your name was Hannah. May I address you by your name, or is there a title I should use? I don't wish to be impertinent. Apparently that is one of my flaws. I am endeavoring to correct it, but reining in my tongue is a challenge, especially when faced with the duplicity and stupidity of the courtiers surrounding me.*
>
> *I passed my last magic exam yesterday, which means I am now allowed to study combat arts unsupervised. My father is proud; he says I shall lead his army before I ascend to the throne. I believe this is meant as praise, but it frightens me. We have not had a war in many years, and I do not wish to see one in my time. It's good that I passed, though, because now I am allowed to enter the practice arena and won't have to hide the evidence of my practice sessions.*

*Next week I'm going to pick out a grim hound pup. Do you have grim hounds in the mortal realm? I don't think so.*

> *Your friend,*
> *Cadeyrn*

Hannah folded the letter carefully and put it in her desk drawer, atop the first. What must Cadeyrn be like? Were the letters a joke? Who would play a joke on her? At school, Jimmy and Peter poked her with their pencils when they walked by her desk, and Monica sometimes made fun of her for reading too much. But this prank seemed beyond them. She couldn't quite imagine Jimmy putting pen to paper and writing such letters, even as a joke.

Then another letter. And another. Every week for three months, she received a short letter, half a page or a page, the penmanship and wording growing rapidly more elegant.

*Dear Hannah,*

*Bran is now as heavy as I am, yet still quite clumsy, as he is yet a puppy. I have drawn you a picture of him. When he is full grown, he will be nearly the size of a horse. You have those, don't you? Unicorns are smaller, but I think you don't have unicorns in the mortal realm. On the same page you will find my renditions of Spat, Snicker, and Grimble. Grimble is the little imp, and Spat and Snicker are the goblins. Grimble and I played a prank on my father last week, and I was soundly whipped for it. I am rather ashamed of it now, yet I feel I should confess it to you, if we are to be friends.*

*Will we be friends? I have not received any letters from you. I should not be disappointed by this; I*

13

*knew it was impossible for you, and yet I pretend to myself that someday I will receive an answer. Cara has informed me that the prohibition on carrying items from your world to ours includes your letters, so he cannot offer this service to you. Yet I hope you will not mind if I continue to send you my own missives.*

    *Your friend,*
    *Cadeyrn*

Hannah felt her heart flutter at the odd mixture of elegance and childishness in this letter. He did sound a bit like a prince, she thought. Perhaps it was not a joke after all. Who was Cara, though?

She wrote a reply to each of his letters, tucking each one dutifully into the top desk drawer with the corresponding letter from him. Roughly once a week the letters would appear, never when she was looking. Sometimes they were slipped under her bedroom door; other times she found the latest letter on her desk, propped against the ever-changing stack of books.

After three months, she received no more letters for nearly six weeks.

Hannah was consumed by curiosity, hoping against hope every morning that she would find another letter. She turned her room upside down, much to her mother's consternation.

"What are you looking for?"

"Nothing! A letter. I should have it, but I don't."

"Well, what does it look like?"

"A letter, Mom. It's fine. I'll look for it myself."

"Don't you want help?"

"No. Thanks, though."

Her mother looked anyway, bemusedly helping Hannah turn over everything in her room, looking beneath books and behind her desk. Hannah cried at night, when the lights were off. Her friend was gone. Perhaps he had never existed at all, though the letters in her desk remained as proof. Proof of a hoax, perhaps, but proof of something, anyway.

The creamy paper of the envelope caught her attention immediately as she struggled in the door, just returned from a weekend at her grandmother's house. She barely suppressed a cry of excitement and opened it right then, her bag dropped at her feet.

*Dear Hannah,*

*I have been forbidden from writing to you; my tutor was quite angry and brought the matter to my father, who says that it is not fitting for a prince to converse with a commoner, and a mortal at that. Never mind that mortal blood flows through our veins anyway. You know that Fae and mortals have ever been connected; many of our ancient royalty were born human and became Fae only after long sojourn in our lands.*

*My father's creativity in disciplining me was truly astonishing. I will not soon forget the lesson.*

*Yet, if you consent to receive my letters, I would like to continue. Cara will continue to deliver them, if I wish it; he is sworn to obey me, not my father, and he is a friend as well as a faithful servant. I will brave the repercussions in order to have a friend.*

*Please tell me you are my friend. I try, at all times, to be grateful and do my duty without complaining, because I know that in so many ways I am privileged. Yet I am surrounded by those who want something of me, and I cannot simply be. If I may simply be Cadeyrn in these letters to you, that is a gift I cherish.*

*Your friend,*
*Cadeyrn*

She told him of her favorite books, and her imagined stories in which she was the heroine facing down dragons. She wrote to him about middle school band, her fervent desire to earn first chair flute, and her triumphant exhilaration when she succeeded. She picked up guitar her freshman year of high school and folded a copy of her first songs into the letters he would never see.

> *The goblins somehow managed to set fire to the lower throne room. It baffles me how they accomplished such a feat; the entire room is made of stone. Even the throne itself is inflammable. Yet flames licked the ceiling, and it took nearly an hour to put it out.*

> *They are such inventive creatures. It is fortunate they are well-nigh indestructible.*

His letters followed his life, telling of fears and joys, triumphs, failures, disappointments. He frequently enclosed a page or two of his drawings. His goblins were hideous little creatures, bulbous and leathery. Some had wings like bats and triangular mouths full of needle-like teeth. Others were lean, with long, oddly-jointed legs and cat-like whiskers sprouting from beneath elephantine ears. The imps reminded her of leprechauns, tiny little men with irritable expressions, sometimes holding a tiny scythe or a wisp of something she couldn't identify. Fairies looked much like she'd expected, though there were apparently two kinds, those with dragonfly wings and those with butterfly wings.

The centaurs were her favorite, though he drew few of them. Comonoc was their king, and Cadeyrn's drawing of him showed not only his exquisite beauty, but noted in a corner that Comonoc was one of the few courtiers that Cadeyrn trusted. Hannah pondered that for a while, examining the masculine face and torso atop the equine body.

*I find myself disappointed once again in my father. Perhaps I am wrong to write this, because he is my king and I do not wish to convey any disrespect or disloyalty. Yet his actions cause strife with the troll king and his allies, including the king of the Unseelie, and I fear he will drive us to war.*

The artless simplicity of his earliest letters faded into a kind of tentative courtliness, as if he meant to be intimate but couldn't quite remember how. Sometimes, when she entertained the thought that he was real, that his words were truth, she wondered whether he was tentative because he was unsure of her, or whether he guarded his words because he thought his letters might be intercepted.

*Dear Hannah,*

*I went to the mortal realm for the first time last week! It was fantastic, much more exciting than I had been told. I went to a place called Beijing. Is your home like Beijing?*

*I have been given approval to grant mortal wishes now. They are not binding on me, yet there is some satisfaction when we do so. Is there some wish I might grant you? If so, I should like to do you some small service in gratitude for the encouragement of your friendship. For I feel, despite your lack of reply,*

17

*that we are friends; the thought of recounting my ac-*
*tions to you has stayed my hand several times when I*
*might have acted... differently. My kind are not prone*
*to mercy, and the royalty least of all. I have known lit-*
*tle of kindness, myself, and yet I feel it is something*
*you would value.*

*I wish... but we only grant wishes. We do not*
*have our wishes granted.*

*I remain your friend,*
*Cadeyrn*

Over Christmas break her junior year of high school, she received a letter that made her question again whether Cadeyrn and his stories were real.

*I wish I could bid you merry midwinter, for it is meant to*
*be a festive time. Yet this year it is far from joyous. War has*
*come. I ride out tomorrow at the head of my father's army. Be*
*well, my friend.*

No letters came for six months.

Hannah flopped onto her bed with a sigh, folding her still-slim arms behind her head. Her hair had darkened a little as she grew so that it was now only a few shades lighter than black.

"Are you packed yet?" her mother asked from the doorway. "The beach is waiting."

"No. Sorry." Hannah mumbled. Shadows danced across her face, and she closed her eyes against the sunlight slanting through the tree branches outside her window. Perhaps he had forgotten her. Perhaps he had never existed at all; perhaps he was only a prank, an invention of one of the bullies who still teased her. Perhaps he had died.

"I wish I knew whether you were real." The words slipped out without thought. She sighed, her heart letting go of the dream she'd held for so long.

Shadows shifted, and she opened her eyes, squinting into the afternoon brilliance. A shape moved on the branch outside, blocking the light for a moment, and she sat up.

The white owl blinked at her, his eyes a glowing, improbable gold. He ruffled his feathers and shifted his feet, then settled down contentedly, still watching her with those striking eyes.

Hannah grumbled to herself, then moved toward her dresser, the empty suitcase already open on the floor.

Propped against her mirror was a creamy envelope. Had it been there before? Surely she would have noticed it. She glanced at the owl as she turned it over in her hands. It didn't look at her, only shuffling its feet a little as it settled down, as if readying itself for sleep.

> *Dearest Hannah,*
>
> *I regret that I have been unable to write you these last months. You must doubt my friendship, if not my very existence. I assure you, I cherish your friendship no less now than before. More, even, for there is little enough of beauty in war.*
>
> *I dare not put much to paper, for the war is far from over. Regrets weigh heavy on me, yet I have done nothing but what I must, and that with as much mercy as was possible. More, perhaps, because I imagined your reaction if I acted in petty cruelty rather than the jealous, righteous, royal anger which is my right and my duty.*
>
> *I never thought to see a centaur weep. I did not think they were capable of it. But we have all done*

*things in these last days that we could not have fore-
seen.*

*I bid you sweet dreams this night and all nights.
One of us should have easy sleep.*
*Yours,*
*Cadeyrn*

It was a year before she received another letter.

*Dearest Hannah,*
*We have won.*
*Yet I am not sure if we have not lost, after all.*
*Cadeyrn*

The following week Hannah left for college. She
wondered whether his letters would find her there, and
to her delight, she found a letter tucked underneath her
pillow that evening. Perhaps he, or perhaps the mysteri-
ous Cara, was more cautious now that she didn't have
her own room. But her roommate never snooped, and
the letters continued.

*Dearest Hannah,*
*The aftermath of war is a trial unlike anything I
might have imagined. The goblins have recovered
quickly, of course; their intellect and nature do not
permit long grieving. Their city is nearly destroyed,
but with some time and effort I can rebuild it for
them. The centaurs have paid most dearly for our victory, but others have made sacrifices as well. Their
grief is deeper, and there is less I can do to ease it for
them.*

*My father turned at the end. He lived long
enough to see the fruits of his betrayal, and it grieved
him. He saved me, I think, though I cannot be sure.*

*I want to believe he did. I cling to the memory, false though it may be. It is the only solace I have, and a poor one at that, because it is built on wisps of magic, smoke and reflection and recollection. I don't want to know the truth. I fear I am not strong enough to bear it.*

*My dreams are plagued by nightmares. Victory is a bitter draught, only slightly less bitter than defeat.*

*Yours as ever,*
*Cadeyrn*

No longer a wobbly cursive, his writing had matured into an elegant script that reminded her of the documents in the old buildings downtown, letters written by well-educated, powerful men. She might almost believe he was a king.

Hannah majored in literature, which fed her soul; she minored in journalism because she hoped to find a job after graduation. With some luck and several unpaid internships, she managed to find a position at an up-and-coming fashion magazine. Although she didn't really care about the name brands, she managed to make a name for herself writing a frugal fashion column. The job was, or should have been, a dream come true; she enjoyed the idea that everyone should be able to afford to feel beautiful.

*Dearest Hannah,*

*It has just occurred to me that I have never sent you a drawing of Cara, though I have written of him often. He is growing old, though I doubt anyone but I can see it. He hides his aches well, as I hide my own sorrows. As I must.*

21

*It falls to me to host the Midwinter Masque. My heart has never much enjoyed these balls, for I feel I wear a mask far too often as it is. Yet the people enjoy them, and my presence is required; to absent myself would unnecessarily cause offense, in addition to alarming the commoners. Far be it from me to deny them this small thing.*

*Winter seems particularly long and dark this year, though I suspect it is only my own feelings that make it that way. Winter in Faerie is longer and darker than in your realm; I suspect time passes differently in many respects, and I am probably older than you are now. I believe it was not always so, or at least the difference was not as great. Perhaps it is a result of humanity's fading belief in Faerie, or perhaps it is only that Faerie is fading.*

*The goblins are afraid of the winter winds and have spent much of the season in the palace. They have been especially destructive lately, and I find myself irritable at their antics. Then I am irritated at myself for being irritable, because they cannot help themselves. They are goblins, and that is what they are and always shall be.*

*I pray you forgive my melancholy.*

*How shall you celebrate Midwinter? I hope you find warmth and the comfort of family and friends surrounding you.*

*Yours always,*
*Cadeyrn*

Hannah sighed as she pondered that last letter. She was lonely too. Now living outside Washington, D.C., she did most of her work online, supplementing her meager salary with an independent photography business. She'd filed the paperwork last year to make it official, and already she was booked. Most of her work was wedding and engagement celebrations, and while she enjoyed sharing in the joy of these personal moments, it had thrown her own loneliness into sharp relief.

She'd wondered sometimes if there was something she lacked, some reason why her coffee dates never seemed to turn into a deep relationship.

This year, for the first time ever, she was not spending Christmas with her parents. It was their thirtieth wedding anniversary, and she'd been delighted when they'd asked if she minded whether they went on a cruise. Just thinking of them on a romantic cruise, dancing every evening and soaking in the Caribbean sun, made her smile.

She swallowed a lump in her throat. At twenty-seven, she felt too old to be lonely for her parents, but the feeling persisted. Christmas wasn't the same without family. Her single friends had all made plans to go skiing. She hadn't joined them; business was good, but not that good yet, not after she'd just bought her little house. D.C. wasn't a single-income town. She faced a week in an empty office before Christmas and a few days off, which she would spend alone.

Hannah flipped to the next page, blinking in surprise at the drawing. Cara was a white owl, sharp eyes turned on her with disconcerting realism. Most of Cadeyrn's drawings were pen and ink, sometimes accented with intense or subtle watercolors. Cara's eyes were a brilliant orange-gold, and she knew, with a certainty beyond all evidence, that she had seen him outside her window.

*Dearest Hannah,*

*Let it never be said that I throw a lackluster ball. I have enclosed some drawings for you. Perhaps they will bring you amusement.*

*Spring comes too slowly for me this year. It would brighten my dark days if I could bring you some small happiness. If you could have one wish, what would it be? Perhaps, if you say it aloud and use the right words, I might be able to grant it.*

    *Yours,*
    *Cadeyrn*

Hannah smiled, delighted in his drawings. Cadeyrn might have been an artist, perhaps a concept artist for a movie studio. The ballroom was filled with elegant figures, slim and radiant in gowns dripping with jewels. Bizarre masks covered their faces; some evoked the grotesque goblins, others seemed more like real animals, birds of prey, deer, foxes, even fish. Lanterns hung suspended in the air, though no chains or ropes supported them. She looked at the next page and gasped. An owl mask stared up at her, hooked beak shaded so that it seemed to emerge from the page. Each feather was meticulously drawn and painted in breathtaking realism. Behind the mask lurked brilliant azure eyes, the pupils mere pinpricks of black against the extraordinary blue. Beneath the drawing, Cadeyrn had written his name.

Hannah licked her lips and sighed, putting the drawings down. She stretched her shoulders and wandered into the living room carrying the newest drawings. She had an arrangement of his art in simple black frames in her living room, and she switched three of the older drawings with these new pieces.

Christmas Eve. She was caught up on all her work and tired of staring at her computer screen. She flopped onto her couch and flicked on the television, finding a familiar movie and smiling at the memory of watching it with her parents. Today, though, it felt empty, and she turned it back off, letting the silence fall around her. She trailed her way to the kitchen and turned on the teapot, heating water for some hot chocolate.

"I should do something festive. Hot chocolate is festive, I suppose."

Outside, the snow that had been promised all week had finally begun to fall, sticking to her little Corolla and glinting on the brown grass in her tiny front yard.

She pulled on a coat and stepped outside, breath fogging in the cold air. She took a few steps out into the driveway and turned to look up at the already-dark sky.

"I wish I didn't have to eat leftover Mexican for Christmas Eve dinner tonight. I wish I'd put up lights. I wish I didn't have to turn on the television for the sound of a human voice. I wish..." her breath caught, and she forced down the sob, turning it into a resigned sigh. "I wish I didn't feel like a baby for being lonely."

A tiny sound in the shadow beside her front door made her whirl.

"I'm sorry. I probably wasn't meant to hear that last bit." The voice was made of layers upon layers, an intoxicating mixture of innocence and sensuality, overlaid with a gentle embarrassment.

A dark figure stepped forward, and Hannah gasped.

He was a king. There was absolutely no doubt of that. A king at ease, but a king nonetheless. He wore dark, slim-fitting breeches of some unknown fabric tucked into knee-high boots. His jacket was long and dark green, a rich fabric lush with embroidery so fine that she barely picked out the subtle shades in the patio light. It hung open in the front, showing a crisp white shirt opened one more button that she would have expected, revealing a triangle of smooth skin. His hair was dark and wild, sticking up at crazy angles.

The patio light behind him caught only the angular line of his cheekbone and jaw, a little too sharp and pale to look entirely human. From the shadow of his face, she caught the gleam of brilliant eyes fixed on her.

"I… you're… you're…" She couldn't breathe. "I didn't think… but you are. How did you… but why… and… really? You are?" She closed her eyes for an instant, wincing at her sudden inability to use words.

He stepped away from the door, deliberately letting the light wash over him. "I didn't mean to frighten you." That voice! She could never have imagined its depth, the sudden stirrings inside when she heard him speak.

"You're Cadeyrn. I don't even…" She frowned, her cheeks feeling hot against the icy air. "I probably don't even know how to say your name right! And you're real? You're him?" She stared at him helplessly.

The pale skin of his throat moved as he swallowed. "It's Kahd-ern. It's an old name." His voice had an odd inflection to it, and she wasn't sure if it was because he was uncomfortable or insulted, or that almost unnoticeable accent, or something else entirely.

He pulled his gloved hands from his jacket pockets and made a gracious gesture toward the door. "You must be cold."

"It's a dream. This must be a dream," Hannah murmured. She drifted toward the door, her heart fluttering oddly as she passed him. A faint scent tickled her nostrils, and she took a deep breath of moonlight, snow, pine sap, and something else, like cinnamon but wilder and colder.

He followed her inside, his steps quiet on the tile floor. She slipped off her shoes, stepped into the kitchen and turned off the stove, then looked up.

"What did you do?" The words escaped without thought, and she stared at her living room.

A tree stood in one corner, dusted with what looked like real snow, although it showed no signs of melting. Candles stood at the tip of each branch, casting a soft glow over the room. Across the mantel of her never-used fireplace was draped some greenery, with bright holly berries peeking out near the base of more candles. Her table was set for two with exquisite white china she'd never seen before and sparkling crystal wine glasses.

She glanced up at him, finally seeing his face in the unforgiving fluorescent light of her tiny foyer. His eyes were the same brilliant blue as in his painting, a detail she'd been sure was exaggeration. The planes of his face were sharp, his cheekbones a little too high. His eyes were slanted, canted slightly upwards like a cat's eyes, and his eyebrows looked… odd. More steeply angled than his eyes, giving them the look of wings.

He swallowed again, his thin lips pressing together. "Perhaps this was a bad idea. I should go." He glanced at the table and one setting disappeared. Silver serving dishes appeared in the middle of the table.

"No!" She watched him, the cautious way his eyes flicked over her face. "Stay, please."

He hesitated, then inclined his head. "If you wish it." His voice had the slightest oddity to it, as if he were mocking her, or himself, or something else entirely. She wasn't sure, and she wasn't sure whether she was meant to be insulted or sympathetic.

"I'm Hannah," she offered.

Those blue eyes sparkled, and the corners of his lips lifted in a tiny smile. "I know." He caught her hand in his gloved one and bowed over it, his lips just brushing her knuckles.

She gestured at the living room. "So... I..." She blinked again, glancing at him. "I thought you must be a fantastic storyteller. Maybe a teacher, with all that talk of goblins." She heard the slightly hysterical edge in her voice and caught her breath. "But... you're real?"

"Evidently." His lips quirked a little more. "As are the goblins."

She studied him again, and he let her, his eyes roving over her as well. His gaze lingered on her lips and her hair, on her hands clenched in an ineffective attempt to hide their trembling. He stood nearly eye level with her, a little short for a man, though his wild hair made him look taller. Power swirled around him, invisible but unmistakable.

"I'm not what you expected," he murmured. "My apologies."

"No! You're..." She searched helplessly for words. "You're fine. Would you..." she glanced at the table, "like to stay for dinner?"

He licked his lips, revealing teeth that were a little too sharp and white. "If you wish it."

She had a moment's misgiving. Her nerves must have flashed across her face, because he took a half-step away from her, adjusting his gloves deliberately, as if to give her time to think. The second place setting returned. He pulled out her chair for her, waiting with gracefully inclined head while she sat. The scent of moonlight and snow, cinnamon and magic, filled her nostrils again as his jacket brushed her shoulder.

"May I?" He indicated her coat rack. At her nod, he slipped out of the heavy jacket and hung it up. His shirt skimmed his lithe body, with slightly looser sleeves ending in wide, embroidered cuffs extending halfway up lean forearms. He did not remove his gloves. It was an odd look, but it suited him; he exuded a wiry, alien strength, his every movement graceful and assured. Then he looked at her across the table, the candlelight falling on his face. His pale lips made a funny, uncertain expression, and she realized he was as nervous as she was. "Is steak acceptable?"

She nodded wordlessly. Within the space of a blink, the serving dishes were gone, and her plate was filled with a perfectly done steak, cheesy potatoes set to the side, asparagus in a neat line beside it. Red wine appeared in the glasses.

He waited until she began before he ate a bite, using the European style of holding his fork in his left hand. After a few moments, when the silence had grown uncomfortable, he cleared his throat. "I haven't had the pleasure of learning about you over the years, so I feel a bit at a disadvantage. Would you tell me of your life? Cara is not often concerned with details."

He asked about her family and her job, expressed an interest in seeing her photographs, and nodded encouragingly at all the appropriate places. She noticed only near the end of the meal how skilled he was at making her comfortable. She found herself chuckling as she recounted some anecdote from her first week at work, and he smiled.

The expression so startled her that she stopped, the words fading in the air between them.

"What is it?" Those absurd eyebrows drew downward a little, lending him the look of a puzzled falcon, all flashing eyes and talons.

She had to clear her throat. "You smiled. A real smile. It was…"

Cadeyrn glanced away. "I haven't smiled in too long. Thank you for giving me reason to." He smiled again, but it was not the quick, unguarded expression of before, laughter and music in his eyes.

There was no washing up; Cadeyrn waved a hand and the dishes disappeared. He watched her walk to the tree in the corner, examining the snow that still had not melted in the indoor heat.

"I took the liberty of assuming you merely wanted lights outside, not that you wanted to travel back in time and install them yourself."

She looked out the window and gasped. The glow of brilliant lights around the window bathed her face, and she saw them lining her tiny patio and the driveway, glittering on the snow.

"They're fairy lights. They'll fade when you wish them away."

Hannah looked over her shoulder, studying Cadeyrn anew. He stood by the fireplace, shoulder leaning on the mantel, arms crossed loosely over his chest.

"You must know I'm not human. So I haven't entirely granted your wish yet."

"You've..." She looked outside again, breathless with wonder. "This is beautiful. What more could I want?"

"You wished that you didn't have to turn on the television for the sound of a human voice."

Heat crept over her face, and she looked down. "I'm sorry."

"For what? Wishing to spend your Midwinter with your loved ones? There is no shame in that."

She glanced up to see a wry smile on his thin lips.

"So I've brought you a gift." He held out one hand, and a tiny blue flame danced over his gloved palm. "A trip to see them, whenever you wish. Next week, if you like, once they're done with the cruise. Leave now, enjoy next week with them, and come back the moment you left. Or tomorrow morning, if you wish to skip tonight altogether."

Hannah studied the flame. "I don't understand. Leave now, enjoy next week, come back to tomorrow?"

"If you wish."

He was watching her, blue eyes bright with intensity that made her breath catch in her throat.

"I have a gift for you too." She bolted down the hall and into her bedroom, where she found the boxes of her letters to him. She picked up the first one and carried it back to the living room. "It's not much, but maybe you'll like it." He'd been looking at the wall of his own framed art, blue eyes glittering with some unreadable emotion. She hesitated, seeing his bizarre, otherworldly beauty. The light caught his dark hair like a shock of chestnut thistledown.

"A gift for me?" he murmured, as if the idea was unfamiliar. "Why?"

Hannah held the box out. He studied her face for a heartbeat, then took the box as if it were something precious. He sat on the sofa, resting the box on his knees.

Cadeyrn ran a gloved finger over his name, written years ago in wobbly cursive on the cardboard lid. He glanced at her, then carefully lifted the lid. Head tilted, he looked at the neat row of envelopes and folded pieces of paper.

"These are my letters. You kept them?" His voice held a hint of wonder.

"Not just yours. Mine too." She pulled the first pair of letters out, his envelope and the folded paper of her reply.

He looked up at her, eyes wide. "You wrote back?" The words were only a whisper, as if he couldn't quite get enough air in his lungs. "I never thought..." He looked back down, and the muscles of his throat worked as he swallowed. "May I keep them? Read them?"

"Well, I'd like to keep the ones you wrote to me." She smiled, putting a hand on his arm for a moment. His muscles twitched beneath her fingers, and she drew back, her face flushing. "But the ones I wrote are yours. I would have sent them if I'd known how."

Cadeyrn nodded jerkily. "Of course. I should have told Cara..."

"I have four other boxes."

Cadeyrn glanced up at her again, eyes inhumanly bright.

"I can sort them for you if you want." She jumped up, bringing the other boxes to the coffee table in two trips.

Cadeyrn ran one gloved finger down the top edges of the envelopes. "No need." He waved gracefully at the corner, and another box appeared. A moment later, it was full of neatly stacked pieces of folded paper and her boxes were half empty. "That is a gift of great value. Thank you." He straightened, his voice a little tight. "And you? My gift seems... inadequate now. Let me think of something else."

"You don't need to do anything else."

He tilted his head, the motion oddly birdlike, his eyes sharp on her face.

She swallowed, feeling her face heat under his scrutiny. "I always thought you must be so brave and so creative, dreaming of such stories. You wrote of war, and I imagined you meant that your parents were getting divorced and you felt alone. I thought you'd grown up to be one of those teachers they make movies about, civilizing the little hellion children with dysfunctional families; I thought you called them goblins to keep your own dreams alive while making the dreams of others come true. You're an artist, with your words and your drawings, and I cherished every letter.

"I thought how kind you were to keep writing to me, when all I did was grow up to write and take pictures of pretty people wearing pretty clothes, even though I don't care about clothes. You never even got an answer! And now I find that it was all real, and I didn't... I didn't realize you were really a king. Because why would a king write to me?" She found herself wiping tears from her eyes, but she couldn't look away from his face.

Cadeyrn blew out a soft breath, his slanted eyes distant for a moment. "The war was very real. I don't know if I'm brave. I doubt I'm particularly creative, since I only wrote the truth. But that was your gift to me." He focused on her again, seeming to consider his words. "Mercy is not... esteemed... among my people. Yet the lack of it cost my father. I wanted to be different, but at every turn, in every moment of every day, I was trained to be ruthless. My father died in the war. I never told you the details." His face tightened, and he swallowed; one gloved hand clenched, then relaxed by his side. "I assumed the throne when I was sixteen; the war was not yet over. I wanted to... move on from the old ways. Reform, if you will. It was a good opportunity because there were so few left to oppose me." His thin lips pressed together in a white line for a moment before he continued.

"At first you were a childhood friend, but you became my conscience. I have such power; it would be so easy to use it poorly. I imagined what you might think, knowing that I would write to you only the truth, not gilding my words with false justifications. Would my friend be disappointed? Would *you* be disappointed in me?" His eyes focused on her with sudden intensity. "My father was feared. I am... respected, I think, and loved, at least by many of my subjects, if not all. I thank you for that."

The enormity of it took her breath away. "But I didn't do anything," she whispered.

"You read my letters. Cara told me that. That was enough." His eyes searched her face, then he murmured, "Thank you." He bowed solemnly.

The silence between them drew longer, until finally Cadeyrn murmured, "I should go."

"I have a wish!" Hannah blurted. "I know what I want, if it's not too much. Maybe it is." She frowned uncertainly.

He tilted his head, eyes bright on hers. "Ask."

She swallowed, watching the candlelight dance on his cheekbones and across his narrow nose. "You said in one of your letters that you never had anyplace you could just be. I wish this could be that place."

He blinked. "That's all?"

"I wish you'd keep visiting." She licked her lips. "And that we could be better friends."

A tiny smile tugged at his lips. "When?"

"Tomorrow?"

Cadeyrn's brilliant smile might have lit the room.

# TWO

H annah woke the next morning with the same sense of expectation and excitement that she'd had as a child. Christmas morning! A morning of gifts, of homemade buttermilk biscuits and bacon and scrambled eggs and fresh oranges, of wrapping paper and tinsel, of warmth, of posing for pictures wearing new Christmas pajamas, of a fire crackling in the fire-place.

She scrambled from her bed, showered, then stood in front of her closet wondering what to wear. Last night, of course, Cadeyrn's visit had been unexpected, and she had barely thought about her worn out jeans and thread-bare long-sleeved t-shirt. Now, in the clear light of a snowy morning, she blushed. A king! Her imaginary friend was not only real, but a king. Yet he was her friend; she knew him from almost a thousand letters over the years. She settled on her nicest dark jeans, a soft green sweater nearly the color of his jacket from the night before, and her favorite brown boots.

She didn't have everything she needed for a proper homemade Christmas breakfast, but she had enough. Bacon and eggs, cinnamon biscuits from a can, frozen orange juice. She got everything ready and set the places on her little table. Then she remembered that she had a tablecloth; she rummaged in the closet until she found it, then decided it wasn't an improvement after all and put it back in the closet. She found a glass vase and filled it half-full of water, dropped a few tiny votive candles in it, fought with the long-necked lighter until she managed to get them all lit, and then picked some holly branches off the mantel and put them around the bottom of the vase.

"Not too bad," she muttered.

Then she waited. The eggs congealed in the pan, and she scowled at them, but she could make more when Cadeyrn arrived.

If he arrived.

"Do I have to wish him here?" she wondered. Would it be rude if she did? Would she be interrupting something?

Her stomach rumbled, and she waited. The cinnamon biscuits cooled, and the bacon sat in its own grease. She picked up a book and tried to read, though it was difficult to focus on the story when she kept thinking Cadeyrn would arrive at any moment.

Noon passed. She made the decision at one o'clock.

"I wish Cadeyrn would come if he wants to," she said carefully.

Nothing happened.

She sat on the couch, her stomach still grumbling, and waited for long minutes before sighing in disappointment.

A knock sounded on her door.

Hannah jumped up so fast she barked her shin on the coffee table and squawked in pain, stumbling gracelessly toward the foyer. She took a deep breath, forcing the grimace from her face and replacing it with a smile, before opening the door.

Cadeyrn stood with one eyebrow raised. "What have you done?"

Hannah felt her face heat. "Nothing!" She smiled awkwardly and stepped back, wincing.

He did not step forward. "I... had hoped we would not lie to each other, Hannah."

She blinked. "Uh..."

Cadeyrn's nostrils flared slightly. "Perhaps I should go. I am... not in the best state of mind to be lied to at the moment. It has been a very long and trying morning already, and I should not wish to say something I regret. Farewell." He bowed sharply.

"Stop! Stop, please." Hannah was shocked. "Seriously, you're going to leave over that? I hit my shin on the coffee table. That's all! I didn't want to make a big deal of it. I'm sorry."

He stared at her, those brilliant blue eyes absolutely unreadable. "And you wish me to stay?"

"Of course I do! I made you breakfast and everything. Even though it's past lunch by now." Her voice trailed away as she studied him. Was it her imagination or did he look even more pale this morning? Something about his face seemed different. Sharper, perhaps. The cold winter sunlight reflecting off the snow made his skin look nearly translucent. Had there been those faint shadows under his eyes last night? Would she have noticed?

"As you wish," he murmured finally.

She held the door open for him and he swept in, trim and graceful. His coat was a deep blue, the embroidery making it stiff as brocade, though the patterns were different than any brocade she'd ever seen. Like water, the subtle colors seemed to shift with his movement.

"I can take your coat," she offered, and he let her slip it off his shoulders. The motion was odd and unfamiliar, like that of a servant or a wife, neither of which was a role she had ever filled.

"You made breakfast?" He gestured toward the kitchen inquisitively.

"This is what I always had for Christmas breakfast growing up. Well, more or less. You'll have to wait a bit, though, I need to reheat everything."

"No need." He followed her and studied the food for a moment, then waved his hand. Everything was suddenly steaming.

"What did you do?" She grinned.

"Magic." The corners of his mouth quirked upward, as if he was more pleased by her reaction than by the act itself. "I turned back time for the food, so it is just as you cooked it fresh." He gestured at the table, and suddenly their plates were filled and the glass tumblers were full of orange juice.

"It's not really a breakfast for a king," Hannah said, as they were about to begin. "But it's what I know how to cook."

He blinked at her. "What do you think a king eats?"

"I don't know. Something fancier." She shrugged. "You can magic anything you want, right?"

He gave her a bemused look but said nothing. They ate in silence, and she studied him surreptitiously. Finally she ventured, "I'm sorry your morning was so trying."

"Thank you." He straightened, politely placing his silverware to the side of his plate. "I ask your pardon for my short temper upon my arrival."

"Do you want to talk about it?"

"Not especially." His plate vanished, presumably clean and put away. He folded his arms across his chest and sighed. "A defector from the Unseelie who was given sanctuary in my court took the opportunity of my absence last even to prepare an ambush for me upon my return. He'd been planning it for years and almost succeeded."

"An ambush?"

"An assassination attempt." He unfolded his arms and ran both gloved hands over his face, then blinked, looking rather startled.

"You weren't hurt, were you?"

Cadeyrn glanced at her, eyebrows drawn sharply downward. "Not seriously. But apparently my lack of sleep is catching up with me in the form of appalling manners."

"I..." She frowned. "I don't even know what you could be talking about. You're so polite you make me embarrassed to open my mouth. I'm just... trying to wrap my mind around the fact that anyone would want to kill you. Why?"

He blew out a soft breath and spread his hands flat on the table, studying them as if they held answers. "Everyone has reasons why they do the things they do. I like to think mine are more noble, but... after the war, we were all awash in blood and guilt. Perhaps he was right." He closed his eyes, and Hannah thought he looked deathly pale, the shadows beneath his eyes too dark.

"Is there anything I can do?"

A ghost of a smile flickered across his lips before vanishing. "You've done so much already, listening to my problems and tolerating my poor courtesy. Tell me, what would you enjoy today? What would make this Midwinter beautiful for you?"

She felt her heart stutter as she looked at him, his intense blue eyes beneath those strange eyebrows, the hard line of his shoulders beneath his crisp white shirt. He looked dangerous, a wild fey creature sitting at her tiny kitchen table, the air around him nearly crackling with power.

He studied her face, then sighed softly. "Sometimes I forget that while you know me, you do not know the whole of me. I have frightened you." He frowned at the table, absently smoothing the tip of one finger over a line in the wood. "Perhaps a walk outside would be acceptable?"

"That would be lovely."

He stood gracefully and looked around. "Do you have a coat?"

She pulled her coat off the coat rack and started to shrug it on, only to stop at his frown.

"Allow me."

She swallowed an embarrassed protest as he slipped her old pea coat on her shoulders with practiced gallantry. Then he pulled his own coat on with a quick, careless ease that didn't quite match the beautiful fabric. She half-expected him to offer her his arm, but he merely opened the door for her and followed her out into the snow.

They walked in silence for some minutes before he murmured, "Do you have a destination in mind?"

"Not really. The fresh air is nice, though."

He nodded and lapsed into silence again, his hands shoved in his jacket pockets and expression thoughtful. She glanced at his face, wondering what he was thinking.

The snow crunched beneath their boots. Finally, after long, silent minutes, he said, "I fear I'm poor company now. Perhaps we should turn back."

She sighed. "I'm sorry. I'd hoped you'd feel comfortable here, and I think… somehow it's just awkward."

"No, the fault is mine. I am considering what to do about the traitor. He's put me in a difficult position." At her inquiring look, he tilted his head and studied her face. "You aren't offended by my distraction?"

"You just had someone try to kill you. It would be strange if you weren't distracted."

He chuckled softly, the sudden smile across his face making her heart stutter. "I suppose you could see it that way. Still, I apologize." He licked his lips, sharp white teeth flashing for a moment. "I seem to be doing that rather frequently. Your patience is commendable."

She snorted, then blushed, wondering how uncouth she must seem to him.

His face took on a distant expression and he hesitated, then said, "I argued for clemency for him, and other Unseelie defectors, before the few remaining Seelie nobility after the war. I had been injured and my authority and decision-making were… not entirely unchallenged. The events of last night bring those decisions into question again."

"Oh." Hannah frowned. Out of the corner of her eye she saw his mouth tighten. "Would you like to head back?"

"I think so."

"You never wrote to me of any of those things," she said.

His lips twisted in a wry smile. "I didn't want to think of them. There was a great deal I didn't tell you, but everything I told you was true. I decided early on that I did not want to give you a… false impression of my virtues. My people think it was mercy that stayed my hand, but I've never been sure whether that is correct. I think I hoped that, if I showed mercy to the Unseelie, perhaps my father would find some mercy." He looked down. "He didn't deserve it, I think, but he needed it, and I wished so desperately that someone would give it to him, even after his death. Perhaps his legacy might be changed, if I acted with enough grace."

"You loved him." It should not have surprised her, but it did. The old king had been brutal to young Cadeyrn. Remembering his early letters with an adult perspective, she could read between the lines of his descriptions to imagine an overbearing, disciplinarian father, concerned more with his own prestige and political machinations than with his gentle, introspective son.

"I did." He glanced at her, and added, "Perhaps no one is more surprised than I am."

Back inside, he asked if she would like a fire, and at her assent, he waved a hand at the fireplace. A blazing fire sprang up, crackling over the logs that hadn't been there a moment before.

He settled on her threadbare couch, looking profoundly out of place, even after shedding that gorgeous coat.

"Would you like a drink?" she asked.

"Are you offering? Or shall I provide something?"

She smiled. "I have milk, cola, orange juice, and... I think that's it. Water, I suppose. I'll get it for you. You don't have to do everything."

"Water, please." His odd blue eyes followed her as she stepped into the kitchen, filled glasses with ice and water, and returned to hand him one. "Thank you," he said softly. "You are very kind." She blushed, and he added in the same quiet tone, "Your presence is restful. I had imagined that, hoped for it, but I had no way of knowing whether it would be true."

She didn't know exactly what to say to that, but he didn't seem to expect a response. After a moment, he turned his gaze from her back to the fire.

"I have not yet had the pleasure of reading your letters to me. Would you tell me of yourself?" he asked. "What do you love? Why do you take photographs of strangers? What makes you… unique?"

"Unique?" She took a deep breath. "I don't know that I am."

He chuckled. "Of course you are. Cara chose you. He is an excellent judge of character. Besides, everyone is unique. I only asked *how* you are unique." The startling, unnatural beauty of his smile took her breath away.

Hannah swallowed hard and tried to focus her thoughts. She began by telling him about her photography business, how she'd started with an interest in landscapes and macro photography but ended up as a wedding and events photographer. "I want them to see themselves as beautiful. So many people don't feel beautiful, you know. I don't. But I think, if we're ever going to feel beautiful, it will be in those moments when we're lit up by the joy and love inside. Even ordinary people become radiant! I want to capture those moments, so they can share them and remember them. I think of them reminiscing years later, laughing about how young they were and falling in love again."

Cadeyrn's gloved hand was raised to his mouth, the dark leather in stark contrast to his pale skin. "Why would you say such a thing?" he breathed.

"Say what?"

"That you don't feel beautiful." He tilted his head, studying her face.

She shrugged, suddenly uncomfortable. "Every girl feels too fat or too short or tall or pale or tan or something. I think it's universal. I'm not complaining."

"You *are* beautiful." It was a simple statement of fact. The intensity of his eyes made her take a short, sudden breath. "Never doubt that." He gave her a tiny, secret smile and looked toward the fire again, as if deliberately letting her regain some sense of equilibrium.

The silence felt awkward, and Hannah glanced at him again, studying the sharp lines of his face, the contrast of the smooth, dark leather of his glove against the intricate white embroidery of his shirt cuff.

Hannah asked, "Why do you wear gloves?"

The very air seemed to stand still around her.

His gaze rested on her, then he gave a faint, defeated sigh. He looked at one gloved hand, fingers spread wide. He turned it to examine his palm. His lips tightened in an expression she couldn't read, then he tugged off the glove, one finger at a time. He rolled his sleeve up above his elbow.

The skin of his arm was the same nearly translucent pearly white of his face, stretched tight over wiry muscle, the paleness marred by long streaks of coal black. A few short stripes on his forearm were overlaid by branching patterns reminiscent of lightning emanating from his hand. His palm was almost completely black, streaks running outwards and up his arm in sharp, spreading angles. The texture of the black areas looked almost the same as the lighter areas, but tighter and slightly inset.

"What is it?" she murmured.

"They're scars."

She looked up at his face, appalled. "Scars? From what?"

He let out a short, sharp breath. "Magic, of course."

She tilted her head, looking at him curiously, trying to keep her expression gentle. When he glanced away, she whispered, "May I touch them?"

His eyes flicked back to hers. "Why?" That one word had such loathing in it that his mouth twisted in dismay. "Forgive me. That was rude. Do as you wish."

She licked her lips, considering carefully before she dared touch his skin. One finger ever-so-gently trailed from the edge of one dark stripe down the branching pattern toward his wrist, over the thin skin of his wrist and the tendons and bones beneath, over the back of his hand following the line zigzagging down the fine bones of his middle finger to his fingernail, then back along another black line, over the tense muscle between his thumb and forefinger, and carefully, softly, clasped his hand in hers, folding her fingers around his.

Only then did she look up to meet his eyes.

"I'm sorry," she murmured. "I didn't mean to embarrass you."

He inclined his head.

"It must have hurt."

Cadeyrn gave a short bark of laughter. "You could say that. But don't worry, not everyone suffers these effects. This was caused by war, not everyday magic."

She nodded, waiting, letting her silence be her question. His hand was warm in hers, perhaps warmer than a human hand.

He gave a soft hm, then murmured, "You want to know more, of course. I should have known." At her nod, he sighed. "What does it look like to you?"

"Lightning, I suppose." She kept her voice gentle.

"I suppose that is the closest approximation to what it felt like, though lightning is fast and this was... more drawn out. My father betrayed our side early in the war and fought on the side of the Unseelie. I refused to believe he meant it; I thought he was playing a long game, as we call it. Deception is practically a sport in the Unseelie court, and while our court is not malevolent as theirs is, we also enjoy our games.

"I was naive. My father had gone to them in earnest and been received with great acclaim. The high king of the Seelie! Of course he was a great political prize to them, in addition to the intelligence he offered. He told them every one of my weaknesses... the fact that I've never been especially good at water magic, the weaknesses in our fortifications, the names and locations of my few friends... there wasn't much to tell, because he had isolated me so, but he told them enough." He glanced at her and added, "Why do you think I never wrote to you during the war? I didn't want to betray you. If he had known of your existence... there is no action that I would have put beyond him."

He looked at the fire, his voice lowering. "The Unseelie king and I faced each other in battle. I was losing, and my father... had a change of heart, I think. Or perhaps I imagined that. I can't be sure, because my memories of the event are shrouded in..." He stopped, closed his eyes, his throat working as he swallowed. "We can manipulate time. We do not have infinite power, but we have some small degree of ability to... shift things. I see possibilities, repercussions, courses of action. With too many people and too much violence and too much magic being thrown around, fire and earthquake and lightning and spear and arrow and sword and knife and *chaos*, I cannot always remember exactly what happened and what only might have happened.

"I woke in a field of corpses. It had been seven days since the battle ended. It was hot. The world was rotting around me. Cara found me that night; he had been searching for days, of course. We had won." His mouth twisted in a bitter grimace. "It cost most of the nobility and even more of the commoners, though the little people were spared." At her curious look, he licked his lips. "The little people... imps, goblins, fairies... small and mostly powerless creatures. Even the dryads fought."

"And you survived," she murmured, looking at her fingers twined among his, black and pearl and cream.

"I suppose," he said in the same voice. Then he cleared his throat and straightened a little. "But I'm sure that's not what you meant to spend your evening discussing." He smiled, and it nearly reached his eyes... nearly, but not quite.

She rubbed her thumb over the back of his hand, then let her fingers slide from his. "What would you like to do?"

He blinked, studying her face. "What do you mean?"

"Well, if you don't have to go back yet, and I hope you don't, we should do something you enjoy."

That smile nearly took her breath away, a look of such utter, startled joy. "I thank you for your thoughtfulness. I should return soon. But perhaps I have time for a quick drawing. Would you mind?"

"Mind what?"

He glanced around, his gaze falling on her bookshelf. "Perhaps you could read while I draw?"

She rose to peruse the bookshelf, considering the titles. "Do you need anything? I only have printer paper."

His voice had a smile in it. "I can 'magic' what I need. Thank you."

Hannah turned to him with a playful frown, her chosen book in hand. "You're mocking me, Your Majesty."

Cadeyrn's eyes sparkled. "Only with the utmost affection."

Heat suffused Hannah's face, and she looked away. His voice suddenly made her tremble, like wine and chocolate and music flowing through her veins, intoxicating and innocent. She sat in her little armchair, pulled off her boots, and drew her legs up beneath her, resolutely forcing her face into a relaxed expression.

For some time, the only sound was the soft scratching of Cadeyrn's pen on paper and Hannah's pages turning at intervals. She'd chosen an old favorite, but found herself drawn into the story anyway, the familiar sentences holding their own magic. Hannah forgot the king sitting a few feet away.

"I must leave you now. Thank you, Hannah. It has been a most pleasant day."

Hannah looked up to see Cadeyrn rise, a faint grimace flashing across his face at the motion. "What's wrong?" she asked.

"It's nothing serious."

She blinked, remembering. "I thought you said you weren't hurt last night? Do you need anything? Are you sure you're all right?"

"Quite sure. Thank you." He handed her several sheets of paper, the pen and drawing board he'd used disappearing from the sofa. "These are for you."

"Will you come again?" she whispered, looking down at the top sheet. Her face stared back at her, a soft smile upon her lips, her eyes filled with gentle kindness. "Is this how you see me?"

"Yes to the second question." He met her eyes. "And to the first, if you wish me to return." There was the faintest question in his eyes.

"Yes. Please do."

"Then I bid you farewell and good evening." He caught her hand and bowed over it, warm lips just brushing her knuckles. "And I thank you for the pleasure of your company."

# THREE

The day after Christmas had always seemed a little strange to Hannah. The presents were all opened, the banquet cooked and eaten. This year it seemed even stranger.

Dressed in flannel pajamas and her robe against the morning chill, she wandered out to her tiny living room. The Christmas tree still stood in the corner, its candles unlit. She started hot water, planning to have some cocoa, and turned back to the tree. The candles looked perfectly ordinary, although they hadn't dripped wax onto her worn hardwood floor. She'd wished them out Christmas Eve and been only a little shocked when they all went dark at once. The next morning she'd forgotten about them until Cadeyrn arrived; at some point during the day Cadeyrn must have lit them, because they were bright when he'd left Christmas night. She'd wished them out again, not wanting them to burn while she was sleeping. Now… would they light?

"I wish the candles would be lit," she whispered tentatively. Her eyes widened with excitement when they obediently flared, the yellow light warming the room. Despite the apparent lack of holders, they sat firmly upright, not wavering or wobbly on the slim tips of the branches. She grinned.

After a quick breakfast, she sat down at the table with a notebook and a pen. She started a letter to Cadeyrn, but then glared at the lined notebook paper. This would *not* do.

She looked up stationery stores online, but there were only a few in her area and none of them were open. She growled in frustration, then started her letter over again.

*Dear Cadeyrn,*

*I meant to write you with nicer paper, but I don't have any and everything is closed. I feel strangely embarrassed about this.*

*It's odd to write to you now, knowing that you might actually read my letter. I can't even remember all the embarrassing things I must have told you over the last however many years. I hope you don't hold them against me, or at least not for too long.*

*I wish I could describe to you how it feels to suddenly learn that magic is real. We live in a world without magic, or at least not the kind of magic that you do. Perhaps you know this already; you told me of your travels to the human world before, although I thought you were speaking in metaphor and not literal fact. Still, I feel I should let you know how wonderful it is to me. How bright and beautiful your world seems! Yet I know you've seen such darkness in it, and the last thing I want to do is minimize that.*

*The Christmas tree is lovely. The fairy lights outside are the envy of my neighbors. Mr. Blackstock across the street has been peering through his window for two days; I think he's trying to figure out how I hid the cords so well.*

*I've always wanted to make a gingerbread house with real gingerbread. My parents and I made houses a few years with graham crackers, but it can't be the same. When you come again, if you do (and I hope you do!), would you enjoy doing that together? I think it might be fun.*

*Perhaps I should have mentioned this earlier, but I wish you would let me be properly sympathetic about the attack Christmas Eve. You may not think it was anything serious, but I saw the look that flashed across your face so fast. You wanted to hide your pain; you were hurt, and you didn't want me to notice. But I wish you would trust me. You may not know me from a thousand letters, but I know you, or at least I know some part of you. I know you're brave, and I know you're kind, and I know you're sad, and I know you're lonely. I can't fix everything for you, but I can be a friend. I want to be. Sorrow is easier to bear when someone bears it with you.*

*I hope you'll come visit whenever you like.*
*Your friend,*
*Hannah*

She pulled on her coat and a fluffy hat before stepping into the light snow flurries outside. Eyes downward, she circled the block before heading down a side street. What did she want from Cadeyrn? He was a friend, of course; though even that felt new and bizarre.

The Cadeyrn she had pictured for years and the Cadeyrn of reality, however magical, only overlapped in their courtly language and artistic talent. In her mind, Cadeyrn was tall with soft, floppy blond hair. A child of a broken home, he'd compensated for that pain by becoming an inspired teacher, the kind who identified and nurtured the most vulnerable little hearts in every class. He spent his leisure time on some obscure hobby like swordplay, or perhaps that was a metaphor for his interest in the debate team. Although she had barely admitted it to herself over the years, she had nurtured a quiet crush on this fictional Cadeyrn, with his charming words and his beautiful drawings and his rich imagination.

Yet... he'd been telling the truth all along, albeit not every ugly detail of the truth. He'd never referred to the war or his father's betrayal in more than passing generalities in his letters. He'd never written of his physical injury in the war, which had obviously been traumatic. He had written only passingly of his mother's death some years before; Hannah had the impression that she had been broken by her husband's betrayal.

How well did she really know Cadeyrn?

She thought of his pale, sharp face, the caution in those piercing blue eyes, his startled expression when she'd suggested doing something he would enjoy. He didn't expect to feel happiness, didn't expect to have his preferences taken into account. What a strange kingdom he must rule.

Hannah watched her breath fog, the tiny clouds disappearing almost immediately as the snowflakes drifted down. Cadeyrn was utterly different than she had imagined. Yet the feelings she had carefully ignored for so many years had flared in his presence. She closed her eyes and thought of his voice; she might have fallen in love with him for that alone. Or was that lust? She grimaced and stuffed the thought down.

Back at her house, she stomped the snow from her boots and brushed the flakes from her hat and shoulders before opening her door.

A letter rested on her dining room table, just beside her own letter. She spun, looking for Cadeyrn, but the room was empty. She strode to the window. A white owl perched on a branch, almost invisible until it moved.

"I bet you're cold," she murmured. She opened the window. "Would you like to come in?"

The owl tilted his head, and studied her with those great, golden eyes. Then Hannah had to jump back from the window with a startled squeak as his flew in, great wings barely clearing the window frame. He perched on top of her bookshelf with a satisfied mutter, shuffled his feet and fluffed his feathers, then stared at her.

> *Dearest Hannah,*
>
> *I hope I may still address you as dearest, now that you have met me. I am not the selfless teacher of children you imagined, nor am I the spinner of fictional adventures who might have captured your imagination. I am only Cadeyrn. I hope you are not too disappointed; I cannot tell, because I am sure that, even if you were disappointed, you would be too kind to tell me to my face. So, if you wish to no longer receive my letters, please feel free to tell me in a letter at any time. While saddened, I will not be offended. The actuality of my existence cannot possibly bring peace to your happy life, and I do not wish to cause you distress.*
>
> *Nevertheless, as you were so kind as to encourage my continued correspondence, I have thought of a gift you might enjoy. I have been reading your letters,*

*though I have not finished them all yet. In one of them, I believe you were fourteen or so, you mention a desire to see Victoria Falls, which is, indeed, a beautiful sight. Have you ever had a chance to visit it? Would it please you to go?*

*Faerie also has a number of natural wonders, many of which are within my lands. My favorite waterfall has a name that would translate as something like Thundering Diamonds. It is not as wide as Victoria Falls, but it is several times taller, and the rocks surrounding the falls are dotted with diamond and sapphire deposits which glitter in the sun. Perhaps, if you like, I can take you someday.*

*If it is snowing when you receive this, would you look for Cara outside? He has been suffering more in cold weather these last weeks. I think his age and long service are weighing on him more heavily. I won't offend you by offering recompense for any shelter and food you give him, but I would be most grateful if you let him rest a while before he returns to me.*

*With many thanks for your kindness, I remain your*
*Cadeyrn*

The warmth in his words, however cautious, made Hannah smile. She thought for a while, then added a postscript to her letter.

*I just received your letter. As I write this, Cara is taking a nap on top of my bookshelf. I will offer him a snack when he wakes.*

*You are right; you are not at all as I had imagined you. But that does not mean I am disappointed. Far from it. I am sorry that for so many years I didn't realize you were telling me the truth.*

*I had forgotten that I'd written about Victoria Falls, but I've always wanted to go. Your Thundering Diamonds sounds spectacular! I would love to see them with you.*

She hesitated, then signed it *Yours, Hannah.*

Cara slept atop her bookshelf for hours. Hannah nearly forgot about him, busying herself with long-overdue cleaning. At last she flopped on her couch and sighed heavily. "I should make something for dinner." The refrigerator was disappointingly empty of inspiring ingredients, and she sighed again, grumbling to herself. She had eggs left and a few random vegetables; maybe an omelet would be good.

She hummed while she cooked, thinking about her schedule for the weeks after Christmas. She had a wedding photography session booked on New Years Eve, but other than that, she had nothing other than her day job planned until the middle of February, when she would visit her parents.

A soft hoot caught her attention and she looked up. Cara perched a few feet away, his golden eyes intent on her sizzling omelet.

"Do you like eggs? That seems rather… cannibalistic."

Cara tilted his head so far to the side that Hannah had to laugh. "Maybe some leftover bacon would be better." She pulled out the bacon and eyed it, then glanced at Cara, who merely stared back at her with those enigmatic eyes. She crumbled up the bacon into small pieces, then put it on a plate for him with some pieces of bread. He ate it all without stopping.

"Is that enough or do you want more?"

Cara hopped onto the table and looked at the letters.

"Yes, I wrote back. Can you take it for me?"

He tilted his head again. Hannah sighed and walked to the window. She opened it, and Cara swished silently past her shoulder, disappearing into the night.

When she looked back at the table, her letter was gone.

Days passed with no sign of Cadeyrn. Hannah knew she was being impatient, but she couldn't help feeling jittery. She went jogging Saturday morning, more to sweat out her nerves than from any particular desire to get in better shape. The sidewalks were icy but the roads were adequately salted. She dodged chunks of grey snow and tried not to slip, her breath fogging in the air.

Finished with her circuit, she slowed to a walk and trudged tiredly toward her door, eyes on the ground.

"Is this an inconvenient time?"

She looked up to see Cadeyrn standing beside her door. "Oh! No... um... well, I need to get cleaned up. Come in?" she offered.

"Thank you." He followed her inside, graceful and silent.

She pulled off her old running shoes, uncomfortably aware of the sweat scenting the air around her. "I'm sorry; I really should go shower. Do you want anything? Water? Make yourself comfortable."

He tilted his head as he looked at her, those odd blue eyes lingering on the sweaty hair plastered to her temples and frizzing out from her ponytail, on her flushed cheeks. She had the bizarre feeling that she had completely confused him, but she didn't know how, exactly. "I require nothing. Would you like me to leave?"

"No! No, it's fine, if you don't mind waiting a few minutes."

"Not at all," he murmured. He took a half-step back and watched as she hurried down the short hallway to her bedroom to gather her clothes and then slipped into the bathroom.

Hannah showered hurriedly, towel-dried her hair, and pulled on her clothes. She glanced in the fogged mirror, made a face at herself, then stepped out into drier air of the hallway. Silence greeted her.

She walked out into the living room to see Cadeyrn studying his own framed artwork on her wall. He glanced at her and a faint smile flickered over his lips. "You like them?"

"They're beautiful. Even as a child you were very talented, and the more recent ones... well, I always get compliments on them when I have friends over, and then I have to explain that a friend did them, not me." She glanced at him, trying to read his expression. "My imaginary friend."

His eyes sparkled. "Just because I live in Faerie doesn't mean I'm imaginary." He hesitated, then said, "I thought, if you were free, we could visit Victoria Falls this afternoon."

She blinked. "Um... how?"

He held out one gloved hand to her as if asking her to dance.

The weight of the decision, the graceful gesture, the alien beauty of his pale face, made her hesitate a split second, and in that second she saw the sparkle in his eyes fade.

A lump in her throat, she put her hand in his.

"Close your eyes," he whispered.

Then gravity forgot itself for a moment, and she was drifting apart, arms and legs and tendrils of thought spiraling out of control; there was a jolt of stone beneath her feet, and Cadeyrn's hand tightened on hers, strong and steady, his other hand warm on her shoulder.

"Open your eyes."

His words were barely audible over the roar of the water around them. They stood on a tiny outcropping in the middle of rushing water, the edge of the waterfall receding away from them in both directions.

"This is incredible," Hannah breathed, the sound of her voice lost in the thunder. Cool mist swirled around her, whipped in the wind.

For long moments she stood marveling. Her heart soared at the sight, the light dancing on the water, the impossible green of the distant hills, the silvery clouds of spray rising below.

"My presence is required at the palace," Cadeyrn said. "Urgently. Do you wish to return to your home or to accompany me?"

She gaped at him. "I..."

"Decide quickly. You will be safe with me. I swear it." His eyes blazed in the brilliant African sun.

"I'll go with you!" she whispered.

He grasped her hand in his and she closed her eyes, feeling the world shift, fall apart, and reassemble itself in a moment.

Hannah's mouth dropped open.

"This is the lower throne room," Cadeyrn murmured. "Do not be afraid of the goblins. They are loyal subjects of the Seelie court, though their appearance may be... off-putting to you. Remain here, please." He strode quickly across the room, the dark, ugly goblins scuttling and leaping and skittering out of his way with cries of excitement.

The room was large and entirely made of stone, as she remembered he had written to her once. The ceiling soared above her. Light from long, arched windows devoid of glass made stripes across the floor. Near her was a solid stone chair with a high back; it had no padding and no ornamentation other than a line of shallow etching across the top.

Goblins nearly filled the room. The largest were perhaps the size of a large dog, while the smallest could have fit on the palm of her hand. No two were the same shape. Something about their movements made her think suddenly of a room full of rats, shifting and sliding past each other.

She looked for Cadeyrn, fear rising. He stood near the door, frowning as he looked down at a shorter being. A dwarf? He nodded once and continued listening, glancing at her once and then back to the speaker.

The goblins stared at her, whispering and muttering in odd little voices. Finally one of them, a knobby little monster with crooked triangular teeth, sidled forward and grinned. "You're the girl." Its voice was a raspy whine that somehow managed to be both terrifying and endearing. "The one the king loves, yes?"

"Um… I don't know about that."

"The human girl." Its grin grew wider, and its bulbous eyes sparkled merrily. "Yes! You are. The Hannah-girl. Human girl. Wrote the king letters. Cara-Owl flies between worlds and takes king's heart to you in letters. So many years!" He giggled, and the other goblins followed suit.

"I…" Hannah stared across the room at Cadeyrn, who was still focused on the dwarf. Was it true? He'd been so… reserved. But what did she know? How would the goblins know what he thought? "Why would you think that?" she whispered.

The goblins burst into cackling laughter, falling over themselves in fits of giggles. "Why? She asks why? Hahahaha!" One thickset, doe-eyed goblin slapped a smaller, elephant-eared goblin on the back, and it rolled onto its back, feet kicking, still laughing. "Hoohoohoo!"

"Think you the king writes everyone letters?" One little goblin, its spindly legs drumming on the floor, covered its eyes with both hands. "Thinks we don't know but we do. We do! We love the king, we do, and we know things. We love what he loves. Good king, he is. Very best in all that ever was."

The one who had addressed her first finally controlled his laughter, looking at her with twinkling eyes. "We love you, too. Make our king happy, you do."

"I do?"

The creature's grin widened, sharp teeth glinting. Hannah felt a twinge of fear, then stuffed it down when he nodded eagerly.

"Oh, yes." The goblin flicked his wrist and a deep purple fruit appeared in his hand. "Want a plumberry? Very sweet. So tasty!" He offered it to her.

Hannah studied it, glanced at Cadeyrn, then cautiously took the fruit. She examined it again, inhaling an intoxicating, sweet scent that reminded her of peaches, raspberries, and plums. The skin had just the slightest velvety feel, more subtle than that of a peach.

"Thank you," she said finally.

She took a bite.

The sweet juice burst into her mouth, and she nearly groaned with pleasure. The taste was even better than the smell, like sunlight on warm skin. She realized she'd been thirsty from her run earlier and hadn't even thought about it until now, the juice sliding down her throat. She licked her lips, each taste more blissful than the last.

Cadeyrn looked up, his eyes wide and horrified as they fixed on Hannah.

She looked at the fruit, whole in her hand, considering it. Her mouth watered, and she realized she was parched from her run earlier; she hadn't thought about her thirst until now. The juice would be sweet relief. She opened her mouth and brought it to her lips, already anticipating the first delicious bite.

Cadeyrn crossed the room in the blink of an eye and snatched the plumberry from her hand. He bent to growl into the goblin's face.

The goblin squawked in protest, scrambling backward. Cadeyrn snatched him by the neck and held him up at eye level, enunciating something in the goblin language so terrifying that the goblin immediately went limp, eyes closed and mouth locked in a miserable frown. He nodded, and Cadeyrn dropped him unceremoniously to the floor.

"Come," he snapped, and reached for her hand.

"What's wrong with you?" she gasped, pulling her hand away. "He was just being nice!"

Cadeyrn's thin lips pressed together in a grimace she couldn't read, and he grabbed her hand far too quickly for her to pull away again.

Gravity fell away, and so did reality, her constituent atoms spiraling away from each other in a nauseating dance before she snapped back into herself, sick to her stomach and dizzy. She barely kept herself from retching, and she whirled to glare at Cadeyrn.

"What was that for?" She breathed slowly, through her nose, trying to push down the nausea and the rising headache, trying to keep her words in check. She was vaguely aware of having arrived in a sitting room with a marble floor and several couches near an enormous stone fireplace, one wall lit by a row of high windows. But she spared no attention for the room.

Cadeyrn stood swaying, his skin a bizarre shade of gray-purple. His eyes flickered over her face, lingering on her lips.

"I swore you would be safe," he whispered.

Hannah opened her mouth, prepared to… berate him? Protest? She drew in a breath… then stopped. He looked *terrible*. The pallor of his skin had always been strange, but now the gray-violet undertone looked like everything that made him alive had been sucked away, leaving only those burning blue eyes. A trickle of silvery liquid slipped from one nostril.

"You're bleeding," she murmured. "Is that blood?"

He crumpled, falling with a jolt to his knees, shoulders slumping and head drooping forward before he fell on his face. He made no attempt to catch himself; his face hit the stone floor with a sickening crunch.

Hannah felt hysteria rising, her body frozen in place, betraying her. *I'm not like this! I should help him! I should do something!* But what could she do? She closed her eyes, willing her heart to slow its panicked racing, willing her breathing to steady itself.

She carefully turned him over to rest on his back, surprised at how heavy he was. His flesh was firm and warm; if he'd been human, she might have thought he was feverish, because he seemed a little too warm. But he'd been that warm before; at least, his hand had been warm. The silvery liquid had smeared over his lips and across one cheek. She wiped at it with the edge of her sleeve. The flow had already stopped, and that was slightly reassuring.

A larger spot soaked silver-grey on his breeches near his right hip, and she wiped at it, pressing her thumb against the fabric for a moment. Cadeyrn grunted softly without waking, his odd eyebrows drawing together for a moment. She rubbed at the damp area again, frowning when it seemed larger. She covered her mouth when she realized the spot was blood soaking through from beneath his breeches; it hadn't been a drop from his nose after all.

"Oh, Cadeyrn. What have you done?" she murmured. "What is happening?"

He let out a soft breath like a groan, one hand clenching for an instant.

The moment he regained consciousness was obvious. One instant he was boneless on the floor, chest rising with each quick, shallow breath. The next instant he was alien power and beauty, lying supine because he chose to, not because he could not rise.

His blue eyes fixed on her, his expression closed and distant. "I offer my most profound—" His eyes fluttered closed, then snapped open again. "—Apologies. My subjects—" He was breathing too hard, gasping as if he could not get enough air into his lungs, and there was a horrible, rattling wheeze in his chest that she had never heard before.

"Just stop a minute!" she cried. "Explain in a minute. I'll wait. Obviously... I didn't understand something. I don't know what, but it's all right. I'll wait. Just... rest. Please."

Cadeyrn's eyes burned into her, his chest heaving, and then he seemed to agree, or give in; he let his eyes close, and his labored breathing began to slow. The wheeze disappeared after a few minutes.

Hannah thought he might have drifted off to sleep. His face was finally almost peaceful; only those strange eyebrows were drawn down in a faint frown.

Then he sat up, the effort leaving him breathless for a moment. He focused those burning eyes on her, brilliant azure in that stark white face. "My subjects are... misguided. I have... mitigated the effects. They meant you no harm."

Hannah studied him, willing her expression to be gentle. Somehow she knew that her anger had been, if not unjustified, at least unnecessary. "I don't understand.

65

They were just being kind to me. I thought they were… ugly, yes, but kind of cute too. They weren't frightening me."

"Goblin fruit," Cadeyrn murmured. At her confused expression, his mouth twisted in bitter amusement. "I thought you studied literature. There's even a poem about it."

"What?"

*"We must not look at goblin men. We must not buy their fruit."* He frowned at her, the bitterness fading, leaving only exhaustion. "They meant to trap you here. Out of love, of course." He swallowed and closed his eyes, as if fighting faintness. He made a tiny gesture, and a pitcher of water and two glasses appeared on the floor between them. "The poem is wrong. Goblins are not malicious creatures. Destructive, and clever, and mischievous, but not malicious."

Hannah poured them both water and handed him a glass. Cadeyrn's hand shook so badly that he nearly dropped it. She steadied it while he wrapped his other hand around it, the smooth leather of his glove warm against her skin. She looked up to see his eyes on her, intent with some complicated mix of emotions.

"What did you do?" she whispered. "What happened? I ate it, didn't I?"

"Yes." Cadeyrn took a long drink of the water and closed his eyes, his head drooping until his forehead rested against the edge of the cup. She wondered whether he was still conscious. Then he straightened. "I turned back time so that I would notice and stop you eating it."

Hannah swallowed. "So you did it for me."

He tilted his head, that odd but familiar gesture. "Of course. How could I not?"

66

"You don't want me here?" The question slipped out without thought. It was a ridiculous question; she knew that. Despite their many letters to each other, most of which he had probably not read yet, they did not truly know each other.

He gave her a tiny smile that bared a few sharp teeth, his eyes holding hers. "I did not say that." He took a deep breath, carefully putting the cup aside, his hands still shaking. "I would not have a captive queen."

Those burning blue eyes did not leave hers.

Had he asked her to be his queen?

Hannah's thoughts stuttered, skipped ahead, and then paused, irresolute. "I... what?"

"Will you be my queen?"

The silence drew out, long and increasingly uncomfortable. Finally Cadeyrn looked down, the movement stiff and uncharacteristically jerky. "My apologies. I have been... hasty. I will return you to your home as soon as I have the strength." His voice was flat, the intoxicating layers somehow stifled.

"I... I..." Hannah couldn't find her own voice. "I'm sorry, Cadeyrn. I'm just... it's such a big decision. I don't know what to say."

"Nothing is necessary. The misunderstanding was mine alone." He stood, then staggered, half-falling over the nearby couch. His gloved fingers dug into the deep green velvet as he gasped for breath.

"Please sit down," Hannah said. She tried to keep her voice steady, not give voice to the fear threading its way through her veins. She rose, arms out to catch him as he swayed. "Please, Cadeyrn. Come sit."

"I don't need help," he spat. The effect of his words was lost when she carefully wrapped one arm around him, feeling him shaking with the effort of staying on his feet.

He didn't protest again as she helped him around the couch.

"The goblins said you loved me but I didn't know whether it was true," she said.

One corner of his mouth twitched upward, then the smile faded. He rested his elbow on the arm of the couch and then put his temple against his fist.

"So you turned back time so... I wouldn't be trapped?"

"Yes."

"What was the dwarf telling you?"

He blinked. Hannah thought the expression of confusion that flashed across his tired face looked bizarrely adorable. "His village has seen Unseelie riders near their lands twice in the past three days. He requested that a patrol do a sweep of the area."

"Is turning back time always so difficult?"

"No. Goblin fruit is particularly strong, and changes the threads of possibility. By eating the plumberry you wove the tapestry very tightly; I had to rip it apart again." His eyes fluttered closed, then opened. He gave her a faint, gentle smile; it held sadness, but pride too. "It was my honor, after all. Even if I did not mean to ask you to be my queen, I would never trap you here. That is one of the old traditions, one I always despised."

"And you swore I would be safe with you," Hannah whispered, wondering.

"I did." His eyes drifted closed again.

Hannah took the opportunity to study his face. The dark smudges under his eyes stood out starkly against his deathly pallor. He looked sharper and thinner than even a few days before; perhaps it was the light, or perhaps it was an effect of the magic. She glanced at his hip, and the silvery stain on his breeches had spread to nearly the size of her hand.

"You're still bleeding," she whispered. "Your hip?"

He gave a soft *hm*, as if he didn't really mean to answer, then murmured, eyes still closed, "It's all right. It's bound by magic. I... exhausted myself enough that I weakened the binding, but it will heal."

"Can I do anything to help?"

His eyes slitted open and he glanced at her without raising his head. "No, but thank you. Are you hungry?"

She licked her lips, then ventured, "I'm actually in the mood for fruit."

He chuckled, eyes closed. On the table appeared a bowl of various fruits, with a selection of cold meats and cheeses and a bottle of red wine beside the refilled pitcher of water.

Before she rose, she said, "Faerie food won't trap me here?"

"I conjure you human food." He blinked at her, innocent hurt in his eyes. "Did I not say I would not trap you?"

"I believe you. I just want to understand." Hannah smiled. Impulsively, she reached out to touch his shoulder, his muscles firm beneath the crisp fabric. "Thank you, Cadeyrn."

His gaze held hers, the corners of his mouth turning up in a faint, pleased smile. "You are welcome, dearest Hannah."

Then she could see the exhaustion take hold of him, the way his eyelids would stay up no longer. The tiny muscles in his face slackened. She stood, then, taken by boldness she could never have imagined, she leaned over to place a kiss against his temple.

# FOUR

Cadeyrn slept on the couch for hours. At some point he shifted; Hannah pushed a pillow under his head as he slid down to lie on his wounded side, the silvery blood now dried and flaking like mica out of the fabric of his breeches. Hannah hesitated, then pulled his boots off, reasoning that no one, not even a fairy king, could possibly find it comfortable to sleep in knee-high leather boots. Cadeyrn must have been beyond exhaustion; he huffed softly as she removed the second boot but did not otherwise move or speak. His feet were covered in soft woolen socks but looked basically human. Somehow Hannah found that reassuring.

Seeing him sleep was strangely intimate. Awake, he had a fierce, alien beauty, restless power held in perfect control. Asleep, his pale face had a kind of childlike innocence, his exaggerated eyebrows drawn downward as if, in his dreams, he was pondering a difficult question. For the first time she noticed that his ears were ever-so-slightly pointed, as if they had been pinched at their tops. The skin of his cheeks was perfectly smooth, devoid of any shadow of a beard.

Hannah cautiously explored the room, glancing at Cadeyrn at intervals. The marble floor had a faint, shiny smear where Cadeyrn's nose had bled on it, but otherwise was immaculately clean. In front of the unlit fireplace was a thick green rug with an intricate pattern of blue and red around the edges. Unlike the windows in the lower throne room where she had met the goblins, the windows here had clear glass in them; she could hear the muffled sound of wind outside whooshing against the glass and stone. A large desk stood off to one side, the top inlaid with an intricate swirling, symmetrical pattern of different kinds of wood. It was beautiful; Hannah had never particularly thought of furniture as beautiful, but she found herself admiring it for several minutes, marveling at the detail and precision.

An open door beckoned. She stood in the doorway and chewed her lip, wondering whether she dared enter what was clearly Cadeyrn's bedroom. Finally, after another glance at his motionless form, she stepped inside.

His bed was large and carved of dark wood, with a green canopy and curtains pulled back at the corners. She smiled, imagining him enjoying the luxury, then wondered whether he slept with the windows open; nothing else in the room spoke of a man of luxurious tastes. It was a spare, almost spartan room, and the thought made her smile fade into a contemplative look. Another desk stood by the window. Beside the desk sat the box of her letters; one of them was on the desktop, a stone sitting on it as if to keep it from blowing away. She craned her neck, trying to read the words, and finally pushed it flat.

> Dear Cadeyrn,
>
> I'm stressed out of my mind, and I wonder why I chose a major that requires so many term papers. This is stupid. I am stupid. I was stupid to do this to myself!
>
> I bet you're laughing at me. If I were you, I would laugh at me! You're probably above all this sort of pressure. Somehow, although I think we all know it's not true, we all buy into the idea that if we spend one more hour on our essays on Chaucer, we'll get better jobs and somehow have better lives. In ten years, or even five years, will this matter?
>
> Sometimes I love the literature I study. I love the power of words and the beauty of the ideas conveyed, the cutting social commentary and the subversive political statements. But sometimes I feel like I'm living in a dream world, forgetting reality and humanity. My roommate April studies political science and economics; she hopes to work in international development and was just accepted for an internship at a nonprofit. She'll spend the summer in Africa doing something worthwhile. I, on the other hand, have an unpaid internship at a fashion magazine, which seems pretty trivial and pointless in the great scheme of things. Even if it's fun... is that really what I want to do with my life?
>
> I'm pretty sure that whatever you're doing is more important than what I'm doing.
>
> Oh, and Jesse, that guy I mentioned who asked me out to coffee, is a total jerk. He tried to cop a feel before we'd even gotten our overpriced brown swill. I give up on men.

*Wow, what a pointless letter. I shouldn't write to you at 3AM.*

*I should probably stop procrastinating. Goodnight, Cadeyrn. I hope your tomorrow is better than mine.*

*Hannah*

She looked around. One side of the bed had a small table beside it holding a thick book. The title was a swirling calligraphy that Hannah could not even recognize. Hannah glanced back toward the door and realized she'd missed the fact that the wall opposite the windows was a wall of books, the shelves extending to the ceiling. There was an opening in the center, through which Hannah could see more rows of shelves. She walked through, gaping. Cadeyrn's bedroom was a bibliophile's dream, a spartan enclave in an enormous library. Row after row of books greeted her, the titles in dozens of languages. She recognized Cyrillic text, and something Asian, perhaps Japanese, but others might not have been human languages at all.

She returned to check on Cadeyrn, feeling guilty for invading his private sanctum. He had not moved; his face still had that dull gray-violet undertone that made Hannah's heart twist painfully inside her. In the sitting room, one wall had a row of weapons on it, several well-used straight swords of some type and two shorter, curved swords. There was a table topped by glass in one corner, and she looked in it; a number of large coins, like medallions, were arrayed on a velvet cloth beside a series of tiny carvings. She tilted her head, studying them, then returned to the couch near Cadeyrn.

Hannah glanced at him, and, seeing him still sleeping, pulled off her own shoes. She settled on the couch, her head on a pillow where she could see his face, and let her own eyes close.

Hannah woke to the feeling of being watched. She opened her eyes to see Cadeyrn sitting up. His boots were still off, and he rested his head on one hand as he watched her. When her eyes opened, he smiled faintly. "I hope you slept well."

"Yes. And you?" Her voice had an embarrassed squeak to it. The windows were dark, and the room was lit by a series of lanterns and torches along the wall; they must have been magic, because they gave off no smoke, casting bright, warm light over the room.

He blinked slowly, as if turning the question over in his mind. "Well enough," he said finally. "I am not confident that I can take you home yet, so I beg your indulgence for a few more hours." He closed his eyes and took a deep breath, steadying himself. "While you are in Faerie, is there anything you wish to do? Some sight you would like to see?" His face had an odd stillness to it, a mask of expressionless courtesy.

"I…" She stopped and licked her lips, considering her words. "Will I never be able to visit again?"

His head tilted a little, and he opened his mouth, then closed it again. The idea of him at a loss for words startled her; he was always so sure and unhesitating. "I had assumed you would find this an unpleasant experience and not wish to return," he said finally.

Hannah gathered her courage and stood, moving over to sit next to him. There was a drawing board and paper beside him, which she moved aside. She slipped her hand into his gloved one, a gentle, chaste touch, letting their clasped hands rest just above her knee. Hannah spoke without looking at him, resolutely staring at their interlocked fingers, cream and black leather, trying not to let her voice tremble. "I don't know if I'm the right person to be a queen, but I will always be your friend. I would be honored to visit again, if you ever invite me. I'm... I would never intentionally hurt you, Cadeyrn." She glanced up at his face, her vision blurred by unexpected tears. "You're brave, and you're good, and I've always wanted someone like you. I think I've always been lonely for you! Your question terrified me. I've known you most of my life but I've only known you for a week. How can I make a decision that momentous on the spur of the moment?

"And now..." she looked down, unwilling to face him as she said what she'd barely admitted to herself. "I want to invite you to meet my family, but I'm afraid you never want to see me again. You're too polite to admit it, of course." His hand tightened on hers almost imperceptibly. "We never even made our gingerbread house. If there was anyone I'd want to make a gingerbread house with, it would be you." She used her other hand to dash tears from her eyes, still not looking up.

"Hannah," he whispered.

She forced herself to look up, sniffling. There was a strange, lopsided, tentative smile on his face.

"You aren't angry?" he murmured. "At the goblins? At me? I'm... clumsy at these things, I think. I had... hoped, of course, and after ripping apart time, my judgment was not at its best. I had a sense of desperation, knowing I would take you home, and you would wish me away, never to return." He tilted his head, studying her tear-streaked face. "I would never want to make you weep, dearest Hannah." He rubbed his thumb along her knuckles then carefully bent to kiss her hand. "Would you forgive me?"

The lump in Hannah's throat threatened to choke her. "Only if you forgive me for... I don't even know. Everything."

He gave a strangled laugh. "There is nothing to forgive."

Hannah watched him, the way his strange blue eyes studied her, the way his smooth, pale chest moved with each breath.

"Gingerbread, you say?" he murmured.

"If you would enjoy it."

"With you? Of course." His smile wasn't exactly joyful, but it was kind and gentle, and held a tiny, fragile hope.

He gestured at the table and a tray of gingerbread appeared, the warm aroma quickly filling the air. An array of bowls filled with frosting and different candies appeared beside the gingerbread.

Cadeyrn stood, then swayed alarmingly and clutched at the arm of the couch, breathing too quickly. "Your pardon," he whispered.

"I can move the table closer," Hannah offered.

Cadeyrn straightened with visible effort. "I'm not an invalid," he enunciated carefully. Then he glanced at her, a tiny smile dancing over his lips. "But the table does look a very long way away, and I'm not exactly at my best." He sat down again. "Besides, what is the use of magic if I can't use it to move a table?" Despite his light words, there was a strained quality to his voice; his fingers dug into the fabric of the couch as if to keep himself anchored.

Hannah sat down beside him as the table appeared within easy arm's reach. "What's this?" She picked up the drawing board she'd moved aside earlier.

Cadeyrn opened his mouth to protest, then merely sighed, looking away. "A fantasy, I suppose. I was waiting for you to wake and… didn't want to sleep more. I didn't want to miss those last moments of your presence."

The top drawing was hurried, Hannah's figure sketched as she lay curled on the couch. Only her face had much detail, her dark hair pushed messily up above her head. Beneath it was another drawing, this one much more detailed. Hannah and Cadeyrn stood, hands clasped, in front of two magnificent thrones. Hannah wore a gown that rivaled any medieval queen's, richly embroidered fabric skimming her slim waist and enhancing her curves. Her expression was one of regal kindness, a gentle smile for the subjects gathered on the throne room floor. But her eyes were turned toward Cadeyrn, and they sparkled with a secret joy.

Cadeyrn's expression was of fierce triumph, a sharp-toothed grin that made Hannah's heart thud faster. His lean face was transformed; she'd never seen such joy in him. Before him, goblins danced; Hannah could almost hear them giggling and chattering in excitement. Behind the goblins stood centaurs, broad shoulders bowed gracefully to their king and queen. Other unidentifiable creatures lurked in the shadows, but Hannah knew they were friendly, celebrating for their king.

"This is beautiful," she breathed.

Cadeyrn made a tiny sound, and she glanced at him. "I thought so," he whispered.

He didn't mean the drawing.

Hannah swallowed hard. "May I keep this one?"

"Whatever you wish, dearest Hannah."

They fashioned the gingerbread into a house and decorated it with candies. Cadeyrn's hands were shaking, and finally he only watched her work, a gentle, wondering smile on his face. They didn't speak; there was too much to ponder already. But the silence was warm and comfortable, a gingerbread and sugar-scented contentment filling Hannah's heart.

It was too soon; Hannah knew that. But she also knew what her decision would be. Cadeyrn would recover and take her home. She would introduce him to her parents, not because she needed their approval but because she wanted it, and she wanted to share Cadeyrn with them. And she would be his queen, not because she wanted to be a queen, but because she wanted to be *his*. She wanted to be Cadeyrn's.

He was already hers.

# C. J. BRIGHTLEY

C. J. Brightley lives in Northern Virginia with her husband and young children. She holds degrees from Clemson University and Texas A&M. She welcomes visitors and messages at her website, www.cjbrightley.com.

# THINGS UNSEEN

## A LONG-FORGOTTEN SONG
## BOOK 1

## CHAPTER 1

*Researching this thesis is an exercise in dedication, frustration, making up stuff, pretending I know what I'm doing, and wondering why nothing adds up.* Aria swirled her coffee and stared at the blank page in her notebook.

*Why did I decide to study history?* She flipped back to look at her notes and sighed. She couldn't find enough information to even form a coherent thesis. The records were either gone, or had never existed in the first place. *Something* had happened when the Revolution came to power, but she didn't know what, and she couldn't even pinpoint exactly when.

The nebulous idea she'd had for her research seemed even more useless now. She'd been trying to find records of how things had changed since the Revolution, how the city had grown and developed. There were official statistics on the greater prosperity, the academic success of the city schools, and the vast reduction in crime. The statistics didn't mention the abandoned buildings, the missing persons, or any grumbling against the curfew. At least it was later now; for a year, curfew had been at dusk.

She glanced around the bookstore at the other patrons. A man wearing a business suit was browsing in the self-help section, probably trying to improve his public speaking. A girl, probably another student judging by her worn jeans and backpack, was sitting on the floor in the literary fiction section, completely engrossed in a book.

Aria flipped to the front of the book again. It was a memoir of someone she'd never heard of. She'd picked it up almost at random, and flipped to the middle, hoping to find something more interesting than dead ends. The words told of a walk in the forest, and for a moment Aria was there, her nose filled with the scents of pine and loam, her eyes dazzled by the sunlight streaming through the leaves swaying above her. She blinked, and the words were there but the feeling was gone. Rereading the passage, she couldn't figure out why she'd been caught up with such breathless realism.

It wasn't that the words were so profound; she was confident they were not. Something had caught her though, and she closed her eyes to imagine the forest again, as if it were a memory. Distant, faded, perhaps not even her memory. A memory of something she'd seen in a movie, perhaps, or a memory of a dream she'd had as a child.

Something about it troubled her, and she meant to come back to it. Tonight, though, she had other homework, and she pushed the book aside.

Dandra's Books was an unassuming name for the best bookstore in all of the North Quadrant. Dandra was a petite, grey-haired lady with a warm smile. She also had the best map collection, everything from ancient history, both originals and reproductions, to modern maps of cities both near and far, topographical maps, water currents, and everything else. She carried the new releases and electronic holdings that were most in demand, but what made the store unique was the extensive and ever-changing selection of used and antique books. If it could be found, Dandra could find it. Aria suspected she maintained an unassuming storefront because she didn't want demand to increase; business was sufficient to pay the bills and she refused to hire help.

Dandra also made tolerable coffee, an important consideration for a graduate student. Aria had spent hours studying there as an undergraduate; it had the same air of productive intellectualism as the university library, but without the distraction of other groups of students having more fun than she was. She'd found it on a long, meandering walk avoiding some homework. Something about the place made concentrating easier.

Except when it came to her thesis. Aria told herself that she was investigating what resources were available before she narrowed her focus. But sometimes, when she stared at the blank pages, she almost admitted to herself the truth, that she was frustrated with her professors, her thesis, and the Empire itself. She didn't have a good explanation, and she hadn't told anyone.

Something about this image of the forest felt true in a way that nothing had felt for a very long time. It was evidence. Evidence of *what*, she wasn't sure. But definitely evidence.

She finished her homework and packed her bag. She put a bookmark in the memoir and reshelved it, resolving that she would come back later and read it a bit more. It was already late, and she had an early class the next day.

After class there were errands, and homework, and more class, and lunch with a boy who'd seemed almost likable until he talked too much about his dysfunctional family and his abiding love for his ex-girlfriend, who lived down the hall in his apartment building. It was a week before she made it back to Dandra's.

The book was gone.

Dandra shook her head when Aria asked about it. "I don't know what book you mean. I've never had a book like that."

Aria stared at her in disbelief. "You saw me read it last week. It was called *Memories Kept* or something like that. *Memory Keeper*, maybe. Don't you remember? I was sitting there." She pointed.

Dandra gave her a sympathetic look. "You've been studying too much, Aria. I'm sorry. I don't have that book. I don't think I ever did."

Aria huffed in frustration and bought a cup of coffee. She put too much sugar and cream in it and sat by the window at the front. She stared at the people as they came in, wondering if her anger would burn a hole in the back of someone's coat. It didn't, but the mental picture amused her.

Not much else did. The thesis was going nowhere, and the only thing that kept her interest was a line of questions that had no answers and a book that didn't exist.

Was the degree worth anything anyway? She'd studied history because she enjoyed stories, wanted to learn about the past. But the classes had consisted almost entirely of monologues by the professors about the strength of the Empire and how much better things were now after the Revolution. Her papers had alternated between parroting the professors' words, and uneasy forays into the old times. The research was hard, and getting harder.

The paper she'd written on the Revolution, on how John Sanderhill had united the warring factions, had earned an F. Dr. Corten had written "Your implication that Sanderhill ordered the assassination of Gerard Neeson is patently false and betrays an utter lack of understanding of the morality of the Revolution. I am unable to grade this paper higher than an F, in light of such suspect scholarship and patriotism." Yet Aria had cited her source clearly and had been careful not to take a side on the issue, choosing merely to note that it was one possible explanation for Neeson's disappearance at the height of the conflict. Not even the most likely.

For a history department, her professors were remarkably uninterested in exploring the past. She scowled at her coffee as it got colder. What was the point of history, if you couldn't learn from it? The people in history weren't perfect, any more than people now were. But surely, as scholars, they should be able to admit that imperfect people and imperfect decisions could yield lessons and wisdom.

It wasn't as if it was ancient history either. The Revolution had begun less than fifteen years ago. One would think information would be available. Memories should be clear.

But they weren't.

The man entered Dandra's near dusk. He wore no jacket against the winter cold, only a threadbare short-sleeved black shirt. His trousers were dark and equally worn, the cuffs skimming bare ankles. His feet were bare too, and that caught her attention.

He spoke in a low voice, but she was curious, so she listened hard and heard most of what he said. "I need the maps, Dandra."

"You know I don't have those."

"I'll pay."

"I don't have them." Dandra took a step back as he leaned forward with his hands resting on the desk. "I told you before, I can't get them. I still can't."

"I was told you could on good authority." His voice stayed very quiet, but even Aria could hear the cold anger. "Should I tell Petro he was wrong about you?"

"Are you threatening me?" Dandra's eyes widened, but Aria couldn't tell if it was in fear or in anger.

"I'm asking if Petro was wrong."

"Tell Petro I did my best. I couldn't get them." Dandra clasped her hands together and drew back, her shoulders against the wall, and Aria realized she was terrified. Of the man in the black shirt, or of Petro, or possibly both.

Aria rose. "Excuse me? Can I help you find something?" She smiled brightly at him.

He stared at Dandra for a long moment, then turned away. He brushed past Aria and out the door without looking at her, and disappeared into the darkness.

Dandra looked at her with wide eyes. "That wasn't wise, but thank you."

"Who is he?"

Dandra shook her head. "Don't ask questions you don't want to know the answer to. Go home, child. It's late."

77677398R00049

Made in the USA
Columbia, SC
03 October 2017